This treasure belongs to

_____

The
Butterfly's Treasure

by

Schim Schimmel

schimmelsmith
publishing

Burbank, California

At the end of summer in a large field of milkweed plants in North America, a young monarch caterpillar eats his last meal before going to sleep.

Suddenly, from out of the warm blue sky, a giant butterfly lands in front of the caterpillar.

It's an old majestic monarch. His wings are tattered with age, and their bright colors have faded.

The old monarch looks around and asks, "Are you the last of this season's caterpillars?"

"Yes sir, I am," answers the young caterpillar with great respect. "The others have already gone to sleep."

"And I am the last of last year's butterflies," sighs the old monarch. "For twelve months I have flown around the world searching for treasure, Young Caterpillar."

"Treasure? I did not know there was a treasure."

"Treasure beyond belief," says the old monarch. "I have seen it with my own eyes and touched it with my own wings."

"Where is your treasure, Old Monarch? Will you show it to me?"

"I will show it to you, Young Caterpillar. But first let me tell you where I have flown and what I have seen."

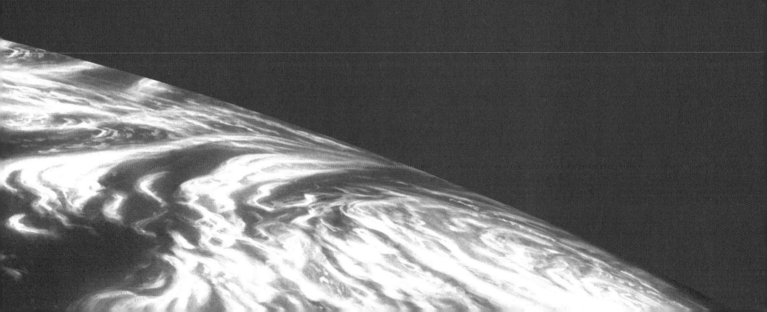

"After waking up and drying my wings, I flew north. Soon the flat, grassy plains turned into giant forested mountains. While flying through the forests I saw for the first time large, powerful animals called bears."

"I flew farther and farther north, leaving behind the mountains and forests. Now there was only ice and snow, and the winds blew cold. There were bears here, too—giant, white polar bears. Sometimes I would warm my wings in the steamy breath from their noses."

"I found beautiful little harp seal pups rolling on the frozen ground."

"This part of the world was beautiful but too cold for a monarch butterfly, so I flew south for many weeks to a continent called Africa.

I was tired from my travels and landed on a small hill to rest. The hill began to walk—I had landed on an elephant!"

"This is where the 'king of the beasts' live, called lions. One time I flew too close to the lion cubs. They chased me and swatted at me with their large paws, and I barely made my escape!"

"Later that evening as I flew past,
I heard the father lion talking to his youngest cub.

He was telling him about the treasure."

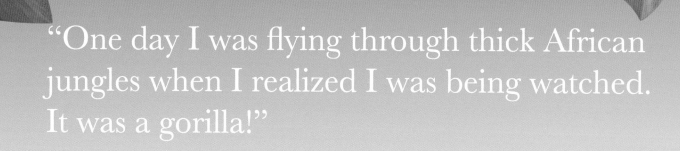

"One day I was flying through thick African jungles when I realized I was being watched. It was a gorilla!"

"He looked huge and fierce, but he was really quite friendly, and only wanted to keep munching on his leaves like you, Young Caterpillar."

"After several weeks in Africa, I flew to Asia to see the tigers I had heard about. Did you know you look like a tiger, Young Caterpillar? They have black stripes, too!"

"Then I searched the Himalayan Mountains in hopes of finding one of the rarest animals of all—snow leopards."

"I only saw a few because they are so shy. Lucky for me, they are not afraid of butterflies!"

"I wanted to see the bottom of the world, so I flew fearlessly all the way to Antarctica. Gigantic sculptures of ice called icebergs drifted in the freezing ocean.

I saw thousands of strange little black-and-white birds called penguins that do not fly, but walk for miles and miles on the frozen snow."

"Many months had passed and I knew it was time to go home. As I made my way across the Pacific Ocean, I watched the dolphins play and leap out of the water."

"I finally reached North America and my instincts led me back to this milkweed field. Some of the last animals I saw on my great adventure were packs of gray wolves running through the woods."

When Old Monarch finishes his story, Young Caterpillar is amazed. But then he remembers, "Wait a minute, Old Monarch, you never told me where you found your treasure."

"But I have told you, Young Caterpillar. Don't you see? This entire world is your treasure, and all its living creatures are its jewels."

Young Caterpillar thinks about this.

"In fact," continues Old Monarch, "our planet earth is the most magnificent treasure in the entire universe."

"And I am one of its jewels!" says Young Caterpillar, all excited.

Old Monarch smiles. "Now you know where to look for your treasure. But first it is time for you to go to sleep."

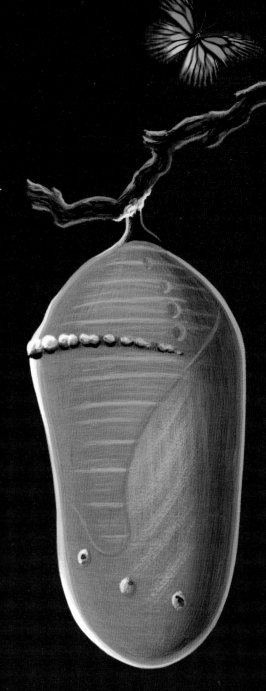

Young Caterpillar makes his bed. As he drifts off to sleep he hears Old Monarch whisper, "This world is your treasure, this world is your treasure, *this world…is…your…treasure…."*

When he awakens, Young Monarch stretches
and dries his damp wings, then looks around.
The old monarch is nowhere to be found.

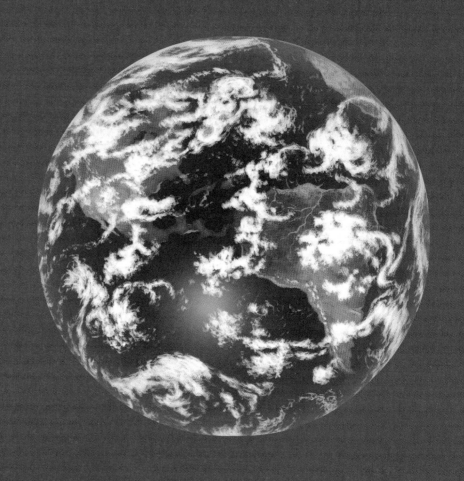

Young Monarch spreads wide his magnificent, brilliantly colored new set of wings. He begins to beat them slowly at first, then faster and faster. He lifts up, up, up into the deep blue sky, a dazzling jewel in the treasure of earth.

The Butterfly's Treasure

Schim Schimmel

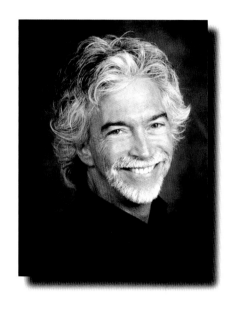

The message behind Schim Schimmel's artwork is the concept of planetary interdependency. "All animals, all ecosystems, all people are intimately connected," says Schimmel, "and together, make up this precious planet we call earth."

Schim Schimmel has been a full-time professional artist since 1987. His paintings and fine-art prints are marketed in Japan and the United States, and his images are licensed worldwide. He is the artist/author of six books including three children's books, and three art books of his collected works.

You can learn more about Schim at www.schimmelsmith.com.

Layout and design by Kirk Smith and Schim Schimmel

SchimmelSmith Publishing
7575 San Fernando Road
Burbank, CA 91505 (818) 252-4330

Library of Congress Control Number: 2009927826
ISBN: 978-0-615-29509-1

Printed in Singapore